This book belongs to:

The Wolf
Who
Cried Boy

The Ugly Wolfling

Wolf
and the
Beanstalk

Of Wolves & Men

Lord
of the
Wolves

Cindawolffa

The
Gingerbread
Wolf

Romeo and
Wolfiette

To Dan,
Tom & Sarah –
for their footprints in the snow.

First published in Great Britain in 2007 by Andersen Press Ltd.,
20 Vauxhall Bridge Road, London SW1V 2SA.
This paperback edition first published in 2008 by Andersen Press Ltd.
Published in Australia by Random House Australia Pty.,
Level 3, 100 Pacific Highway, North Sydney, NSW 2060.
Copyright © Mei Matsuoka, 2007
The rights of Mei Matsuoka to be identified as the author and illustrator
of this work have been asserted by her in accordance with the
Copyright, Designs and Patents Act, 1988.
All rights reserved. Colour separated in Switzerland by Photolitho AG, Zürich.
Printed and bound in Singapore by Tien Wah Press.

10   9   8   7   6   5   4   3   2   1

British Library Cataloguing in Publication Data available.

ISBN 978 1 84270 733 3

This book has been printed on acid-free paper

Footprints in the Snow

mei matsuoka

Andersen Press

It was a cold winter's day.

Wolf sat by the fire in his cosy little house,

reading all the books he had about wolves.

All the wolves in the stories that he read

were **nasty,**

SCARY

and **greedy.**

"I think it's time somebody wrote a story about a **NICE** wolf," he said.

So he sat down at his writing table and picked up a pen. And this is how the story went...

One winter's morning,

it snowed and

snowed and snowed and snowed.

When it finally stopped snowing, a Mr Nice Wolf stepped out of his house to go for a walk.

In the silk-smooth bed of snow, he spotted some footprints leading into the forest. "Hmmm, I wonder whose those could be?" he thought.

He decided to follow
the footprints to find out
who they belonged to, so that
he could make a new friend.

After a little while, he
saw a squirrel in the tree.
"Excuse me, sir. Are these
footprints yours?" he asked him politely.
"No," answered the squirrel. "Why do
you ask?"
"I want to find out so that I can make a
new friend," explained Mr Nice Wolf.

"I don't believe you," said the squirrel. "You just want to find out so that you can EAT the poor thing!"

And with that he scampered off.

Next, Mr Nice Wolf came across
a bunny rabbit poking her nose out
of her burrow. "Excuse me, madam.
Are these footprints yours?"
he asked her cheerfully.
"I want to find out so that
I can make a new friend."

"I don't believe you," said the rabbit.
"You're just hungry and you want
to find some BREAKFAST!"
And with that she hopped
back down into her burrow.

Mr Nice Wolf (who wasn't feeling too nice at all by this point) tried to ignore what she said and carried on. He soon came to a big lake in the middle of the forest.

CROAK, CROAK!

"Oh, could these footprints be yours?" Mr Wolf asked the frog.

"No," said the frog. "And there's no way I would tell you whose they were, even if I knew!"

Then he dived into the lake and swam off.

Right over on the other side of the lake,
Mr Wolf saw a big, brown duck.

"Hello there!"

he shouted.

"These must be YOUR footprints!" he said.
"Yes," answered the duck, swimming over.
"Oh good! I've been looking for you," said
Mr Wolf. "I was hoping we could be..."

And as he spoke Mr Wolf took a good, long, look at the duck and forgot all about what he was saying.

For the duck looked so fat, juicy...

and mouthwateringly TASTY...

Wolf was startled to find himself back in his own house!

"**Pheeew!**
I almost let my story end
with **Mr Nice Wolf** being
just as bad as all the
other wolves!"

Wolf got out of the
bath to dry himself
off when suddenly
there was a knock
at the door.

Wolf called.

He opened
the door...

And in the silk-smooth bed of snow, he spotted...

some footprints! "Hmmm. I wonder whose those could be?"